IS THE SOLDIER SURVIVED

BHARGAVA REDDY
CHINTHAREDDY

"*I would like to dedicate this book to the Indian Army, Navy and air force who fight for the mother nation of India.*"

"*I would also like to dedicate this book to the army of all countries that try to protect their mother countries.*"

ᗷᗷᗷ

Contents

Contents

Preface

The story is about a soldier who is isolated from his troops while helping them to retreat from war. How the isolated soldier survived in the enemy territory for about a few days. What did the isolated soldier do in that 48 days in the enemy territory and how did he help his country in the next war by sending the enemy territory data to his country. Later in the war how he reunited with his troops and helped the war.

ᙠᙠᙠ

Acknowledgements

I here hereby pledge that my work is genuine and isn't copied from any other sources. Everything in this book is fictional and is not based on anyone's life.

ᗡᗡᗡ

Prologue

The story is about a soldier who is isolated from his troops while helping them to retreat from war. How the isolated soldier survived in the enemy territory for about 48 days. What did the isolated soldier do in that 48 days in the enemy territory and how did he help his country in the next war by sending the enemy territory data to his country. Later in the war how he reunited with his troops and helped the war.

ONE

INTRODUCTION

There was a nation called Askalida which was a prosperous nation with a good military. There was another nation called Zanderenia, which is a bigger nation than Askalida and always has a quarrel with Askalida and is always at war. In between these two nations, there was a forest full of large trees and the slopes are good for snipers. At the borders of the two nations at the end of the forest on both sides of the nations. Alex a resident of Askalida went to the military through military procedures and he was ranked last amongst the batch of trainees. After two years of training in the military and he was sent to the battlefield as a backup troop. In an unexpected event of a Zanderenia attack, Alex stands back and helped his troops retreat and infiltrated Zanderenia for his survival and to help his nation.

ᗐᗐᗐ

TWO

CHARACTER'S

Alex - the main character
Askalida:
Higgins - Colonel
Steven - Major
Emanuel - Hacker
Anderson - spy
Dandy - General
Zanderenia:
Bruce - Zanderenia's hacker
Luna - Zanderenia's military cadet
Daniel - Zanderenia's citizen
Thomas - Zanderenia's General
Christine - Zanderenia's Major
Elli - Zanderenia's citizen

ႦႦႦ

THREE

JOINING MILITARY

Alex is an orphan from a small town and always wanted to go into the military as the head of the orphanage was a retired major from the military. He always tells the kids about his adventures in the military and from him, Alex gets motivated and wants to join the military. After Alex reached the age of 18 he went to the military recruitment and got selected as he was training for the military from his childhood. After getting into the military training he works hard for getting a better rank among trainees and frequently gets punished by trainers.

After 2 years of training in the training ground, Alex is sent to the military regiment as a proficient soldier. He was ranked as a lieutenant under Colonel Higgins's regime. Colonel Higgins placed Alex under Major Steven. Major Steven trains Alex more than other soldiers in his regiment. After a few days, Alex got good at sniping, using firearms and melee combat. In major Steven regime, Alex met Emanuel who is a great hacker and both of them became good friends with each other.After a few days, colonel

Higgins sends Major Steven's regiment as a backup for the troops that are present in the ongoing war. After they reached the warzone. The war came to end with a defeat and the backup team got attacked by Zanderenia troops, as soon as Alex saw them he started shooting at them while his regime was retreating and after everyone retreated with some wounds to them, Alex escaped into the forest nearby.

ϷϷϷ

ϷϷϷ

FOUR

ESCAPE

After entering the forest, some Zanderenia soldiers followed him to the forest. After reaching a river, Alex went into the river and hide in the river by swimming downward the stream of the river and escaping from Zanderenia soldiers. After swimming for a distance Alex came out and climbed a large tree and checked for the signs of enemy troops but didn't find any. After some time, he went to the forest to hunt for some food and he found a rabbit. After catching the rabbit he picked some sticks to put fire and he cooked the rabbit after dissecting it. A few minutes after eating the rabbit he climbed the tree to prevent getting caught by wild animals or enemy troops. After finding that there is no threat, he slept on the tree that night and the next day he went deep into the forest and found a cave.

He lived in the cave for about a year While hunting fish, rabbits, etc for food and getting water from the river for drinking purposes. He learned the Zanderenia language from the hunters who entered the forest and got hold of the news of Zanderenia. One day Alex got to know that the Zanderenia military is recruiting people for the military and Alex went into the Zanderenia country by diving into the river from a distance from the Zanderenia country that went into the Zanderenia country from the forest as the security is less there. Alex went into a small village near the border from the river. After that Alex stole one of the recruit's named Daniel certificates and changed the photos and entered the recruitment process of the Zanderenia military. Before entering the military recruitment in the name of Daniel he placed Daniel in an apartment near the barracks and used Daniel's bank account for the money.

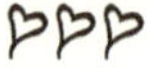

FIVE

MILITARY RECRUITMENT

Alex got good scores in the military recruitment and got praised by the military examiner. After the recruitment examination, the examiner called Alex to the examiner's office and asked Alex how was he so good in the military exams. Then Alex said that he went into the forest for hunting along with his father for their survival and food. Due to that, his survival instincts are high and those instincts helped him in the military examinations. After that, the examiner ordered someone to show Alex his barracks to rest. After reaching the barracks, Alex went to his room and went to sleep after getting fresh up.

In the evening Alex woke up and introduced himself as Daniel and get to know the cadets in his room. After that, all of them went to the canteen and hold a party for entering the military for training. The next day allotment of the department took place and Alex was selected for sniping and his roommate Bruce was selected for the hacking department. Alex made a good friendship with Bruce as he was planning to enter the server room for getting Zanderenia country military information and send it to his country.

ৡৡৡ

SIX
DAY 1

The next day, early in the morning physical training started and most of the cadets that passed the military examination didn't hold up to the end of the early morning training as it was the 1st day of the training. After that, they were allowed to freshen up and for breakfast. After breakfast, all the cadets are sent to the classes and in the classes, they explained the history of the Zanderenia country to motivate the soldiers. After the classes, they were sent to lunch and after lunch, they were given a lecture about the basics of the military. On that day evening again they had physical training for about 2 hours and after that dinner. After the dinner, Alex escaped from the barracks in secrecy and brought a bike and placed it secretly near the barracks. Before coming to the barracks Alex went to an apartment with food and fed it to Daniel and went back to the barracks secretly. After entering the barracks Alex went to his room and went to bed.

ᠵᠵᠵ

SEVEN
DAY 2

The next day early in the morning physical training started and most of the cadets didn't perform like the last day. The examiner punished some of the cadets who didn't do the physical training well. After that cadets are sent to the canteen for breakfast and after that cadets are sent for classes. After the morning classes and lunch, the cadets are sent for physical training with weapons. After that in the evening, they were left free and Alex went out and went to the apartment, with food for Daniel. After that, he went to roam around the city to remember and understand the routes of Alderla city. After the completion of roaming the city, Alex called Bruce on phone and asked him to get his food to the room. After that, he went to a bar for a drink and made a relationship with the bartender. After drinking, Alex went back to the barrack and had dinner in his room. After entering the room Bruce asked Alex where did he go and Alex said that he went to meet his girlfriend. After some time both of them went to bed.

ɒɒɒ

EIGHT
DAY 3

The next day early in the morning, physical training for the cadets started as normally as daily and the cadets got better and better during physical training. While some of the cadets got punished for not doing the training in time or doing wrongly. After that cadets had breakfast and after that, they had classes about basic military combat training. In the afternoon after lunch, the cadets had physical training like every day with weapons and after training, Alex went into the Alderla city. After coming out of the barracks, Alex takes food to the apartment, where he held Daniel and from there he went to the same bar that he went to last night and orders some alcohol. After having alcohol Alex went to a hotel and had dinner. After that, he went to the barracks and asked Bruce for a walk and discussed some technical stuff about computers and servers. After that, about some personal stuff and training. After the discussion, both of them went to bed nearly at midnight.

NINE

DAY 4

Early in the morning physical training started and on that day in the training, Alex and Bruce didn't 'perform well and got punishment due to lack of sleep last night. After breakfast, in the morning classes is actual combat against the trainer and Bruce got hurt and sent to the infirmary for rest. Alex takes lunch to Bruce and after lunch, all the cadets had physical training on the last day. After the training, Alex went out and bought some food for Daniel and give it to him in the apartment. After that Alex took the bike and roamed the different routes of the city where he roam the last day. After that, he went to the bar and ordered alcohol as usual and asked the bartender for information about hunters who hunt in the forest for a living. The bartender showed some people in the bar and said that they were hunters that he asked. After that Alex went to them and asked about the procedure for entering the forest for hunting outside the country walls. After that, they explained everything about the procedures and Alex said that he will pay the bill for them for that day to make friends with them and invited them for dinner. After paying the bill for all of them, Alex and the others went to a hotel and had dinner. After dinner, Alex went back to the barracks and the others went back to their houses. On the way to the barracks, Alex brought some fruits and gave the fruits to Bruce who is in the infirmary and went to his room to rest.

ᐩᐩᐩ

TEN

DAY 5

Early in the morning, the physical training started as usual and some of the cadets got punishment for not performing well. After breakfast, the morning classes were actual combat against the trainer and Alex performed well and got a good impression from the trainer. After lunch, the noon classes are about shooting and physical training. After the classes, Alex went to Bruce to see how his condition was and Bruce said that he is gonna be fine in 2 or 3 days. After that Alex went to the apartment where he hold Daniel to give him some food. After that, he went to roam the Alderla Alderla city where he never went. After roaming the Alderla Alderla city he went to the bar and ordered the bartender some alcohol as per usual. After a few minutes, he searches for the hunters and didn't find them. Alex asked the bartender about the hunters that he met last day then the bartender said they went out for a hunt and usually go for a week and sometimes more than that. After that Alex went to the barracks early than every day and went to the canteen for dinner and after that, he went to Bruce and had a small chat with him. After talking with Bruce he went to bed.

❧❧❧

ELEVEN

DAY 6

Early in the morning, the physical training started as usual and some of the cadets got punishment for not performing well. After breakfast, the morning classes were actual combat against each other. After lunch, the noon classes are about shooting and physical training. After that Alex went to see Bruce and both of them had a chat. After that, he went to the apartment where he holds Daniel like always with food and later went to a store nearby and brought some charts and pencils and went back to the apartment. In the apartment, he draws the routes of the city for his escape route and from there he went to the bar to have some alcohol. After that went back to the barracks to have dinner and after that, he went to bed.

 PPP

TWELVE
DAY 7

From the morning to the evening everything was like usual and Bruce got discharged from the infirmary as his condition get better. Alex asked Bruce to wait for him when he was going for dinner. After that Alex went to the apartment with food for Daniel and draw the map of the routes for his escape. After that, he went to the bar to have some alcohol and in the bar, he saw the hunters who he asked the bartender about previously. After seeing them Alex went to them and asked about their hunt this time and they said the hunt wasn't that good. After hearing that Alex asked them why and they said the military is preparing for war and prohibited and forced them to return. After hearing that Alex asked them when is a war going to be started and they said they don't know. After that Alex left the bar and went to a restaurant and ordered some food and went back to the barracks. After that Alex went to his room and hold a party for Bruce's recovery along with his roommates. After the party, everyone went to bed.

THIRTEEN
DAY 8

As usual, the daily training and classes are completed by the end of the evening and after that, he went to the apartment with food. After that, he went to a mall and brought a new mobile And made a call to Emanuel after going to an isolated area. After Emanuel picked up the call Alex asked Emanuel to give the phone to Major Steven and Emanuel said Major isn't available there and gave Alex Major's number. After giving the major's number to Alex, Emanuel asked Alex where he was until now and Alex said he will explain everything later. After the call with Emanuel, Alex called Major Steven and said that he was Alex and the major didn't believe Alex and asked for confirmation. To confirm that he is Alex to the major he said the code word used in his regime and asked him to call Emanuel for confirmation and said that he will call him tomorrow evening if he believes that he was Alex. After that, he went to the bar and on the way, he met his examiner and invited him for a drink. Both of them went to the bar and had some alcohol and while drinking Alex asked the examiner if there was any war ongoing and the examiner said that no wars were going on and war may occur in a few days. After that, both of them went to a restaurant and had dinner and after that Alex went to the barracks and the examiner went to his home.

ӘӘӘ

FOURTEEN

DAY 9

From the morning to the evening everything is as usual and after the classes in the evening, Alex went to the apartment with food for Daniel. After that, he called major Steven on the phone and asked him did he had confirmation about him. Major said yeah man and asked him how he survived that attack. Alex said that he will explain everything later and asked the major if they are planning for the attack and the major said yes. After that, Major asked Alex how did he know and Alex said that he got the information from his superiors in Zanderenia country. Then the major said that the attack they are planning is in secrecy and many officials in the military itself don't know. After that Alex ended up with the Major and called Emanuel and asked him whether can he hack the Zanderenia country's network?. Emanuel said he can with the help of his department if the major agrees to that and also said that it will take about a day to create a bug that needs to hack the network. Then Alex asked Emanuel to create such a bug and ask the major to stop the war they are going to plan. after that Alex went to the bar and from the bar, he went to the barracks after having some food.

❧❧❧

FIFTEEN

DAY 10

From the morning to the evening everything is as usual and in the evening Alex went to the apartment with food for Daniel. After that Alex called Major Steven on the phone and asked him whether the war is stopped or not and the major said the higher-ups are discussing that and asked Alex to file about how he survived and Alex said he will do it later and cut off the phone. After the call, Alex asked Daniel about the sewage lines that lead outside the Alderla city and Daniel said that he didn't know and Alex tied him again and left. From there, he went to the black market for information and in the market, he enquired about how to escape from this country through sewage lines. They said about the route and Alex brought a map of the route, a laptop and some drives. After that, he went to the bar and from there back to the barracks after having some food on the way.

ᗞᗞᗞ

SIXTEEN

DAY 11

From the morning to the evening everything is like usual and Alex went to the apartment with food. After that, he went to a net café and filed how he survived to Askalida military through his official login ID and from there he went to the riverside. By sitting on a bench he called Major Steven and said that he filed how he survived through the official website. Major Steven said that the war is going to stop and asked when is he returning to Askalida. Then Alex said soon and cut off the phone with Major Steven. After that, he called Emanuel on phone and asked about the hacking of the Zanderenia servers. Emanuel said that it is a bit problematic and difficult but if we install a bug on the server it's gonna be easy. Then Alex asked Emanuel to send the bug to his mail and he will install the bug into the server. Then Emanuel said he will send the bug tomorrow and Alex said to inform the major and end up the call. After that, he went to the bar and had some alcohol. In the bar, the hunter team that Alex met previously is preparing for a hunt the next day and Alex asked them about the war. they said the war is stopped for the time being. After that Alex went to the barracks after having some food on his way back.

❦❦❦

SEVENTEEN
DAY 12

From the morning to the evening everything is like usual and Alex went to the store on his way to buy a new sim and modem for internet on his way to the apartment. After going to the apartment Alex opened the laptop and connected to the internet and opened his mail to check for the mail from Emanuel but he didn't find it. After that Alex called Emanuel on the phone and asked Emanuel about the bug he asked about on the last day and Emanuel said it was ready and that he was waiting for his call. Emanuel sends the bug in the mail while talking with Alex on phone and Alex asked Emanuel for instructions then Emanuel send another mail that contains the instructions for the bug installation. After that Alex cut the phone and transferred the bug to a Pendrive from the laptop after installing it on the laptop. After that, he went to the bar to have some alcohol and in the bar, he met a beautiful girl named Elli and had a chat with her and left to the barracks after having some food on his way to the barracks.

❦❦❦

EIGHTEEN
DAY 13

Early in the morning training is conducted as usual and as everyone going to have breakfast the examiner said that all have to attend the training ground by 9 AM after breakfast. By 9 AM everyone gathered on the training ground and after a while a higher ranking officer came and announced that two days later nation formation celebration are going to be done in the academy. After that, the in charge of the training announced that all the cadets have to prepare the stage and food and everything for the occasion. After the announcement, Alex met the in-charge and asked the in-charge that he would like to do the electrical work with Bruce and the in-charge agreed to him. After that Alex asked Bruce that he want him to download some images of the cities on the national website and he will get some images from the Alderla city with a camera. After that Alex went out and take some photos of the Alderla city that explained the beauty of the Alderla city by noon before lunch. After lunch, both Alex and Bruce made a video from the photos by adding the national anthem as a background and went to the in-charge to show the video. After seeing the video in charge accepted and liked the video and allowed them to play the video on the nation formation day. After that Alex and Bruce went to the stage to check the electrical connection and they had dinner after the checking and went to bed.

❦❦❦

NINETEEN

DAY 14

Early in the morning, the training started as usual and after the training everyone had breakfast. After breakfast, everyone went to different places to work on the arrangements for the nation formation day and Alex sneaked into the server room while making the electrical connections to the stage as the stage is near the server room. After entering the server room Alex took out his mobile and connected to the server and installed the bug from his mail through the mobile. After installing the bug Alex sneaked out of the server room and smashed his mobile and went to work as if nothing happened. After some time Alex and Bruce went to a restaurant for lunch and from there he went to a store and brought the latest mobile in the market. After that, he went back to work and Alex asked Bruce to play the video on the stage for the trial purpose and Bruce played the video. After that in the evening, Alex mailed Emanuel that he installed the bug on the server and instructed him to activate the bug. After that Alex had dinner and went to bed.

ꕥꕥꕥ

TWENTY
DAY 15

Early in the morning, training started and after the training everyone had breakfast. After breakfast, the examiner called everyone and introduced Major Christine who is going to be the in-charge of tomorrow's welcome event. After the introduction, the examiner appointed Alex as an assistant to Major Christine till the end of the event and Alex showed how the preparation are going on for the event. Major Christine asked Alex to show her the cadets who are going to be in the welcome parade for the event and Alex take her to the ground to show the cadets who are preparing for the parade. After that Major Christine ordered the cadets to perform the parade and sorted out errors. After sorting out the errors Major Christine ordered the cadets to perform the parade again and she sorted out mistakes again and again until the evening.

In the evening Major asked Alex about some bars near the barracks and Alex take her to the bar that he daily goes to after taking the bike from the examiner. In the bar, both of them had some alcohol and from there both of them went to a restaurant for dinner. After dinner, Alex dropped back Major Christine at her stay and went back to his room and take his laptop and went to the open area. After that Alex made a video call to Emanuel and asked about the completion of the hacking. Emanuel said that the hack was done and downloading the information from the server is in process. After that Alex end up the call with Emanuel and hacked the surveillance camera network and deleted the footage clip of his entry into the server room. After clearing the evidence Alex went to bed.

ᵖᵖᵖ

TWENTY-ONE
DAY 16

Everyone awaited nation formation day has come and everyone is busy with their work. Alex and Major Christene are waiting at the front entrance to receive General Thomas and high-ranking military officials with the cadets. After some time General Thomas and high-ranking military officials arrived at the front gate and Major Christene, Alex and other cadets salute General Thomas and other officials. After salutation, Major Christene ordered the cadets to divide into two groups. In the two groups, one group follows her lead and leads the official to the stage while parading and the other group will be under Daniel's(Alex) lead and follow behind the official. After reaching the stage all the cadets are on standby and Major Christene ordered Alex to start the event and Alex signaled Luna to start the program. Luna started the program with the National anthem and called the officials to stage based on their ranks.

After that, Alex took the host place and asked General Thomas to have a few words with the cadets about his great achievements on the battlefield to encourage the young cadets. General Thomas said a few lines about his achievements and after the General Thomas word, Alex asked General Thomas to play the video that both Alex and Bruce prepared. After seeing the video General Thomas appreciated all the cadets and after that some officials spoke a few words to boost the morale of the cadets. After that General Thomas hosted the flag and said a few words about the nation. In the meantime, while General Thomas is speaking about the nation Alex went to the canteen to check the food and beverage. After the completion of General Thomas's words, the major Christene asked General Thomas and other officials to have lunch in the canteen and all of them went to the canteen. As soon as General Thomas and other officials entered and had a seat in the canteen Alex ordered the cadets to serve the food in order and all of the officials had their lunch. After lunch, the official went back to the military base and in the event,

Alex saw Anderson a Major rank official in the Askalida military while serving the food. After seeing him Alex took some photos of Anderson secretly. In the evening Alex went to the apartment with food for Daniel and called Emanuel and asked him to check whether Anderson is present or on leave that day. After checking Emanuel said that he was on leave and after hearing that Alex ordered Emanuel to check the spies from Zanderenia in Askalida and cut off the phone. After the call with Emanuel, Alex called Major Steven and said that Major Anderson is a spy from Zanderenia and said that he sent the photos of Anderson attending the Zanderenia's nation formation to Major Steven by mail. While putting Alex's call on hold Major Steven checked his mail and said that Alex did a great job. After that Alex said that he and Emanuel installed a bug in Zanderenia sever and Emanuel is getting the information of spies from Zanderenia. After that Alex cut the call with Major Steven. After that Major Steven sent the photos to colonel Higgins and colonel Higgins sent the photos to General Dandy.

After seeing the photos of Anderson's general Dandy ordered that Anderson is deprived of his status and imprisoned. For the brave actions of Alex and Emanuel both of them are promoted to Captain rank and Major Steven is promoted to lieutenant colonel and ordered to keep the news about Alex was alive a military secret. After getting the news Emanuel called Alex and said the news to Alex. After that Alex went to the bar and had some alcohol and went to a store to buy a watch for Bruce. After that Alex went to the barracks after having some food on his way back. After entering the room Alex gave the watch to Bruce as a gift on the nation's formation day. After that, both of them went to bed.

ppp

TWENTY-TWO
DAY 17

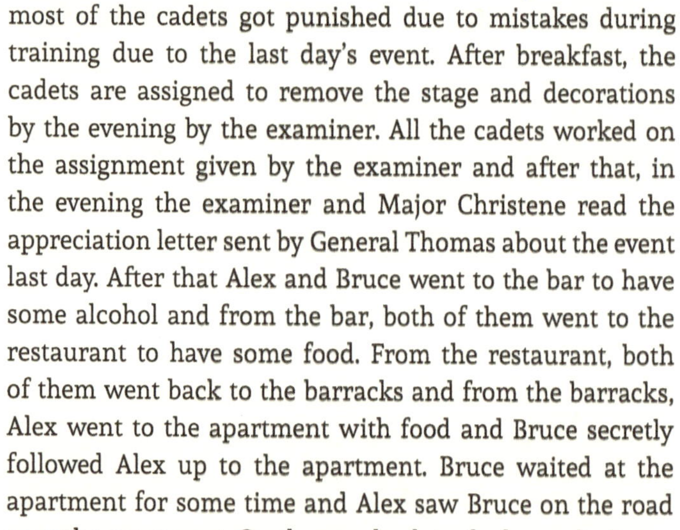

Early in the morning like every day training started and most of the cadets got punished due to mistakes during training due to the last day's event. After breakfast, the cadets are assigned to remove the stage and decorations by the evening by the examiner. All the cadets worked on the assignment given by the examiner and after that, in the evening the examiner and Major Christene read the appreciation letter sent by General Thomas about the event last day. After that Alex and Bruce went to the bar to have some alcohol and from the bar, both of them went to the restaurant to have some food. From the restaurant, both of them went back to the barracks and from the barracks, Alex went to the apartment with food and Bruce secretly followed Alex up to the apartment. Bruce waited at the apartment for some time and Alex saw Bruce on the road near the apartment. On the way back to the barracks Bruce brought a mobile for Alex and installed a software to monitor the phone every day. After Alex comes back to the barracks Bruce gave the phone to Alex as a gift and takes Alex's old phone. After that, both of them went to bed.

ﻌﻌﻌ

TWENTY-THREE
DAY 18

Early in the morning before training, Alex deleted all the data in his previous phone that Bruce take from him last day by using his laptop. After that Alex went to training along with the cadets and everything from the morning to the evening is as usual. After the training in the evening, Alex went to the apartment with food and from the apartment, he went to the bar to have some alcohol. In the bar, Alex met Elli again and had a chat with her and invited her for dinner at the nearby restaurant. After that, both of them went to a restaurant and had dinner. After the dinner, Alex dropped Elli at the apartment where he holds Daniel. Alex went to the flat where he held Daniel and made a phone call to Emanuel and asked about the hacking of the Zanderernia server. Emanuel said that the hacking is going smoothly and found all of the spies from Zanderenia and all of them are imprisoned by the military officials. After that Alex cut off the call with Emanuel and went back to the barracks and went to bed.

TWENTY-FOUR
DAY 19

From the morning to the evening everything is like usual and in the evening after training, the examiner announced that the cadets are going to the military base for a week and from there to the border for about a week. After hearing the announcement Alex went to the black market and brought a gun along with a silencer and gloves. From the black market, he went to the apartment to collect his mobile phone because Alex gave his phone to Elli before he went to the black market. From the apartment, both of them went to the bar and had some alcohol and from the bar, both of them went to a restaurant to have some food. On the way to the restaurant, Alex saw Bruce and invited him to join them for dinner and all of them went to the restaurant. After the dinner, Alex asked to go back to the barracks while he drop Elli back at her home. Bruce went back to the barracks and checked the locations Alex went to that day and found nothing. After dropping Elli at the apartment Alex went to the flat where he held Daniel and killed him with the gun he brought from the black market. After killing him Alex burnt all the details related to him in the flat in an isolated area on the way to his barracks. After entering the barracks Alex handed over the bike to the in-charge as he took it from him a few days back. After that Alex went to bed.

ᚦᚦᚦ

TWENTY-FIVE
DAY 20

Early in the morning After training and breakfast, all the cadets are assembled at the ground for roll call. After the roll call, all the cadets are ordered the board the vehicles that are going to the military base. After all the cadets boarded the vehicles started and after a few hours, all the vehicles reached the military base. After reaching the military base all the cases are ordered to line up fast for roll call and after roll call, all the cadets are sent to the rooms for rest. In the evening before dinner, all the cadets are asked to assemble on the ground for the announcement and as soon as all the cadets assembled on the ground 6 majors along with Major Christine came to the ground. After the Majors came to the ground Major Christine announced that all the cadets are divided into different groups under them for the whole week that the cadets are going to stay in the military base. After that, Major Christine announced that the cadets under which major they have to work and report for the whole week. After that, all the cadets had dinner and went to bed.

TWENTY-SIX
DAY 21

Early in the morning, all the cadets are assembled for training before breakfast and after breakfast, all the cadets are sent to the respected Majors that they are assigned. Alex and Bruce both of them are assigned to Major Christine and Major Christine assigned Bruce to the computer team and Alex to the sniping team under her and the remaining cadets to their respective training teams under her. After assigning all the cadets Major Christine some tasks to complete by the evening and if anyone fails in the tasks no dinner for them and left. Alex was tasked to standby mode in a sniping position for 30min for every hour. Most of the cadets including Alex didn't perform well and got punished. In the evening at the time of the report, Major Christine punished the cadets who failed to complete the assignment to do 59 laps around the ground instead of cutting off the dinner as it was the first day for them. After the punishment, Alex went to the canteen to buy some alcohol and food. After that in the room, Alex, Bruce and some other cadets had the alcohol and food. Suddenly, higher-ups came for inspection and punished all of them to do 100 laps around the ground early in the morning. After that, all of them went to bed.

❥❥❥

TWENTY-SEVEN
DAY 22

Early in the morning Alex and his roommates all did 100 laps around the ground while other cadets are doing training. After the laps, all of them joined the training with the others before breakfast. After breakfast, all of the cadets are assigned to their respective places on the last day and Major Christine gave tasks to complete on that day and if anyone fails the task 100laps around the ground. By the evening most of the cadets performed well and a few got punished. In the late evening, Alex called Major Christine and requested her to have some alcohol in the room as most of the cadets are tired and feeling uneasy due to the morning training and Major Christine permitted with a condition that they won't do anything wrong. Alex agreed and all of them had some alcohol and food that Alex brought in the evening on his way to the room. After having the alcohol and food all of them went to bed.

ﻉﻉﻉ

TWENTY-EIGHT
DAY 23

Early in the morning, all the cadets had physical training and a few got punished due to mistakes. After breakfast, everyone is assigned to perform the tasks that they are assigned like the last day. In the evening Alex got a call from Elli and Elli said that in her apartment the police found a dead person in his flat and Elli said that the police took the information of him from her. After hearing what Elli said, Alex consoled Elli not to worry about him and cut the call. After a few minutes, Alex was called to Major Christine's chamber and Alex went to the Major Christine chamber. After entering the chamber Major Christine said that a case was filed against him and he has to go to the Alderla city police station and report to them. After that Alex went to the city and brought a bike to go back to Alderla city. After that, he went back to base and packed all his luggage. While packing his luggage Bruce asked Alex what happened and Alex explain everything that happened that day from the Elli call to Major Word's and went to bed.

ρρρ

TWENTY-NINE

DAY 24

Early in the morning by the time, everyone is going for training, Alex started his way back to Alderla city as per Major Christine's order to go to the Alderla police station. By noon Alex reached the Alderla police station and after Alex went to the police station, Alex went to the in charge of the case. The officer interrogated Alex about the body found in his flat and Alex said that he didn't know anything and he was away from the last few days. After that, the officer asked Alex why did he buy a flat when he was staying at the military barracks. Alex said that he buy that flat for enjoyment like doing a party or having some alcohol etc., as parties and some other things are banned at the barracks. After a few questions, Alex was released from the interrogation. Before sending off Alex, the officer take his details and ordered him not to leave the city without their permission. From the police station, Alex went to his flat and got fresh up. After that in the evening, he went to Elli's flat and invited her for a drink and both of them went to the bar and had some alcohol. In the bar, Alex met the hunters that he had met previously and had their contact information. After that, both Alex and Elli went to a restaurant to have dinner and after dinner, both of them went to the apartment. After going to the apartment Alex went to his flat and went to bed.

ᎦᎦᎦ

ᎦᎦᎦ

THIRTY
DAY 25

In the morning, Alex went to the market and brought some vegetables and fish. From the market, he went to the store to buy some packed food that should be sufficient for a few days and went back to the apartment. Alex prepared his breakfast and after breakfast, he went to the black market and brought a gun, a sniping gun and twin short daggers with dagger holders. After that Alex went back to the apartment and invited Elli for the home cook lunch in the Afternoon. After that, Alex prepared lunch for both of them with his cooking skills before noon and prepared some wine. After some time Elli came and both of them had their lunch. Elli appreciated Alex's cooking skills and after that, Alex brought the wine and both of them had that wine while having some discussion. After the discussion, Elli went back and Alex packed the packed food and maps in a bag. After packing he left the flat without saying goodbye to Elli or anyone. From the apartment, he went to a small alley and from the alley, he went to the sewage treatment line underground for his escape route. In the evening the police officers went to Alex's flat to take him for interrogation but didn't find him. After finding that they tried to call him and the call didn't get connected. After that, the higher-ups called Major Christine and informed her about Alex's escape. Then she said she will inform the higher-ups and get back to the next day and ended up the call.

ᎶᎶᎶ

ᎶᎶᎶ

THIRTY-ONE
DAY 26

In the morning after the training hours, Major Christine called Bruce to her chamber and asked Bruce, whether Daniel(Alex) called Bruce on the phone and Bruce said no. After that, Bruce asked Major Christine why she asked him about Daniel(Alex) and she said everything that happened in the past few days. Then Bruce said that he can check Daniel's (Alex) gps coordinates. Then Major Christine ordered to do it fast and while bruce is checking out Daniel's(alex) gps coordinates, Major Christine got a call from the Alderla city police officer and the officer said that the dead person was the real Daniel and the one who was in the military was an imposter and cut off the phone. Major Christine relayed the same to her higher-ups and asked for instructions. The higher-ups ordered them to check whether he was a spy or a terrorist. Major Christine ordered the computer team under her to check Alex's identity and send his photo to all the teams by sending a photo of him. After that Bruce checked for Alex's gps coordinates and said that he found Alex's gps coordinates and informed Major Christine about Alex's gps coordinates. Major Christine sent the Alex gps coordinates to the police department. After a few minutes, the police officer called major Christine and said that there was a phone at the location. After a few minutes, Bruce hacked into Alex's phone to get the call data and some other information as he already installed a software previously on Alex's phone. But didn't find anything in the call data and found a document that states that he was promoted to captain level for his contributions to the country with the Askalida country symbol and stamp. Major Christine informed everything to her higher-ups. In the meantime, Alex hides and moves in the sewage lines to escape from the police. In the evening Alex called Emanuel and finish the hack as soon as possible and said that he got into trouble and cut off the phone.

ÞÞÞ

THIRTY-TWO
DAY 27

In the morning, the higher-ups ordered Major Christine to contact the spies and get the information of Alex. When Major Christine called Anderson but the call didn't get connected. After that, Major Christine ordered her computer team to look for the international calls for the last few days in Alderla city and after a few minutes, Bruce said last day a call has been made. Then Major Christine ordered to find the number and exact location of the number. A few minutes later, Bruce said that the number is not working and sent the last location to Major Christine. Major Christine send that location to the Alderla police officers and ordered them to catch him soon. After a few minutes, the police officer called back to Major Christine and said that they can't find any information about Alex there and cut the call. After that, Major tried to call Anderson again but didn't get connected and asked the computer team to check did the server for hacked. After ordering the computer team, Major Christine tried to call the other spies but didn't get connected. After that, Major Christine informed everything to higher-ups and the higher-ups ordered her to call Red. As per the higher-up's orders, Major Christine called Red on the phone and asked why didn't Anderson and everyone's phone didn't connect. Red said that all the Zanderenia spies in Askalida got arrested at the same time as they exactly know they were spies. After the call, Bruce informed Major Christine that all of the Zanderenia servers were hacked by a bug. Major Christine ordered the hacking team to fix the bug as soon as possible and informed all the matters to higher-ups. In the meantime, Alex went to the next city by escaping through the sewage lines outside the city.

THIRTY-THREE

DAY 28

In the morning, Alex went to the city and searched for the information about the black market location and went to the black market for buying some stuff. In the black market, Alex brought a satellite phone, some ammo and information about the city routes, sewage routes and secret routes. After that, Alex went to a small village near the city to avoid the police inspections. In the meantime, Major Christine got a call from a soldier in another regime that he knows Alex. Major Christine asked the soldier to say how he knew Alex then the soldier met him on the battlefield a year ago. On the battlefield, Alex alone stood against 50 soldiers and hold them back until his teammates retreated from the battlefield. After his teammates retreated, he escaped into the forest and finished around 30 scouts who are after him after he escaped into the forest. After hearing all that Major Christine was in shock and cut off the call. After that, Major Christine called Red and asked about Alex's information. Red said that he was in training for about 2years and on his first mission he went missing. After that, Major Christine cut off the phone. After that, Bruce asked Major Christine who is Red and she said Red was a mercenary named

Angelina who is working as a spy on the Askalida country.

♥♥♥

THIRTY-FOUR
DAY 29

In the morning all the cadets who are in training are informed that they have to move back to the barracks from the base. At noon Major Christine got a call from Alex and Alex said that he already escaped from the Zanderenia. Alex thanked Major Christine for letting him out of the military base as an accused without any security and said a few words to major Christine. While Alex was on call Major Christine ordered her subordinates to track down the caller's location. After saying all the things that he wants to say Alex said Red and cut the call. Major Christine called Red on the phone but didn't get connected and the team that Major Christine ordered to track down the caller information that called her on the phone and the call is a satellite call from Askalida country. After that Major Christine relayed all the information that she gathered to the higher-ups and asked for their command.

♥♥♥

THIRTY-FIVE
DAY 30

In the morning all the cadets are sent back to Alderla and after that, all the majors and above rank officers are called for a meeting. In the meeting, General Thomas explained everything and ordered all of them to have to be prepared for war as all the spies in Askalida have been captured. So they don't know when the war might be starting. After that, he showed a document that has been sent by Askalida stating that they will send all the spies from Jakinda back. After discussing some strategies for the upcoming war the meeting was dismissed. In the meantime, Alex went to the black market for information about escaping the country with the military and police officers noticing. In the black market, one of the traders said that it would be possible but the cost is high. Alex asked the trader how much does he require and paid the amount that the trader asked. After receiving the payment, the trader asked Alex to come back at night and went back and prepared his luggage. As per the requested time, Alex went to the black market. After a few minutes, the trader came to the black market and asked Alex to get into a cold storage truck that is used by the hunters. After that, they started moving.

IS THE SOLDIER SURVIVED

♡♡♡

THIRTY-SIX
DAY 31

In the morning, the hunters opened the vehicle door and said that they are outside the country. Alex went into the forest after getting out of the vehicle and before going into the forest Alex took the contact information of the hunters. Alex went to the cave where he previously stayed because the cave is nearby the lake and is somewhat away from the country border. At the noon Alex called Emanuel and send him his location and asked him to send some land mines. Then Emanuel asked why did he need landmines and Alex said that he escaped from the Jakinda country. After that, Emanuel said that he need to get permission from the higher-ups and Alex agreed to Emanuel's words and cut off the phone with Emanuel. In the meantime, all the Jakinda spies are sent back to the Jakinda along with a notice from Major Dandy stating that they are declaring a war against Jakinda after a few days. Alex called lieutenant colonel Steven and asked the same thing that he asked Emanuel and the lieutenant colonel agreed. After that, Alex went into the forest to search does any scouts are roaming in the forest. After that, in the late evening, Alex hunted some fish for dinner along with packed food.

IS THE SOLDIER SURVIVED

♥♥♥

THIRTY-SEVEN
DAY 32

In the morning Alex went hunting some animals and after that, Alex called Emanuel and he need a terrain bike and some gasoline. Then Emanuel said it will take around two days to get the bike and landmines ready that he asked. After that, he went to the forest to search does any scouts in the forest and found out that many army vehicles are moving toward the battlefield between the two countries. Alex went back to the cave and called Emanuel and asked him if there is any war going on. Emanuel said that no war is going on but the country is preparing for a war in a few days. After that, Alex took some handguns along with some ammo and hand daggers and started moving towards Askalida country in the forest without entering the transport road. On the Alex hunted some small animals for food and went beside the river most of the way. On the way, he took some breaks for cooking and to have some rest. By the late evening, Alex reached almost half of the distance and collected some wood to put on fire. After putting the fire Alex went to sleep on the ground.

ᑭᑭᑭ

THIRTY-EIGHT

DAY 33 (FINAL DAY)

In the morning Alex called on the satellite phone lieutenant colonel Steven and asked him to come to the border gate to help him to enter the country for confirming Alex's identity. Lieutenant colonel Steven agreed with him. After the call, Alex started moving again after having some packed food. On the way, Alex met some scouts from Jakinda and finished off them and took the weapons from them away leaving the bodies alone and informed the Jakinda army to collect the bodies of the scouts through the scout's walkie-talkie. By evening Alex reached the Askalida border and called the lieutenant colonel Steven through satellite phone and said that he was waiting at the front gate and asked him to come to the gate to confirm his identity. After a few minutes lieutenant colonel Steven, went to the front gate and confirmed Alex's identity and took him back to the barracks. After reaching the barracks, lieutenant colonel Steven held up a party for Alex's return. At the party, all the people enjoyed themselves a lot and after that, all of them went to bed.

$\heartsuit\heartsuit\heartsuit$

THIRTY-NINE
BATTLE FIELD

The next morning Alex took a bike and some landmines and went into the forest with some scouts to place landmines at the border forest near the battlefield. Alex asked the scouts to draw a map of the route they went and mark the location of the landmines that they placed. By the evening all the scouts and Alex returned. At the barracks, Alex collected all the maps from the scouts and requested the higher-ups to give the maps to the snipers and the higher-ups accepted Alex's request after a discussion with each other.

The awaiting battle day has arrived and Alex asked the snipers to climb up the trees in the forest near the battlefield and gave the maps of the location of landmines that he and the scouts previously placed. The snipers climbed up the trees and stand in position and as soon as the battle started and the snipers shot at drivers and the soldiers who hold automatic guns. After seeing all that the colonels on the battlefield ordered the soldiers to check and kill snipers in the forest nearby. When the soldiers entered the forest the landmines blasted and a few numbers of soldiers died in the blast. After that, the battle went out for a few days and Askalida won the battle against Jakinda.

About The Author

Bhargava Reddy Chinthareddy

This is the second book that I have ever written and I think it's a great one. I don't know when I'll write the next one. I never say anything like I like to write books or anything because most people know that's a lie. so I will say that if you like my book please read the other books that I write in the future. I would like to thank you for reading my book. I had an accident in 2021 and in march 2022 I started writing the book for some earnings for myself to live. Failures aren't stepping stones to success but barriers that you have to overcome that's what I believe.

Books By This Author

The Lost Blacksmith General

once there was a emperor in an empire that goes by name Heavens land. Which consists of some small

kingdoms. There empire was very prosperous under the emperor rule. The emperor never wages a war

against any other empires even though he can win against them but if any empire wages war against

his empire he will completely defeat them and make their under his ruling. The story of a mighty general

who lost everything in his life and lives alone in wild in search of happiness till his last breath. Did the

general had a happy ending or a sad ending.

The Skirt Chaser

How a businessman loves and gets married. Once there was a good businessman goes by a business

tycoon. He owns different types of businesses worth billions of money. He mostly never attended any

meetings and his personal assistant will take care of most of the company affairs and sends every report

to him by evening. He attends only the important meetings and others that he never attended any

event or anything. Most of the employees and contractors don't even know how he looks only the

board members know him.

ppp